What's the Weather?™

SUNNY DAYS

Elisabeth d'Aubuisson

PowerKiDS press™

New York

For the wise and insightful Victoria Zhou

Published in 2007 by The Rosen Publishing Group, Inc.
29 East 21st Street, New York, NY 10010

First Edition

Editor: Amelie von Zumbusch
Book Design: Julio Gil

Photo Credits: Cover, p. 1 © Frazer Cunningham/Getty Images; pp. 5, 9, 11, 13, 17 Shutterstock.com; p. 7 © Courtesy NASA/JPL-Caltech; p. 15 Photo courtesy of Anja and Stefan Engström; p. 19 © Samantha Brown/AFP/Getty Images; p. 21 © Ami Vitale/Getty Images.

Library of Congress Cataloging-in-Publication Data

D'Aubuisson, Elisabeth.
  Sunny days / Elisabeth d'Aubuisson.
      p. cm. — (What's the weather?)
  Includes index.
  ISBN-13: 978-1-4042-3685-1 (library binding)
  ISBN-10: 1-4042-3685-6 (library binding)
  1. Sunshine—Juvenile literature. 2. Weather—Juvenile literature. I. Title.
  QC911.2.D675 2007
  551.5'271—dc22
                                        2006030157

Manufactured in the United States of America

Contents

Sunny Days

Sunny days put people in good spirits. Many people like feeling the Sun's warmth on their skin. Others enjoy the colors that sunlight brings out. Some people like to lie back and look up at the deep blue sky.

A sunny day is a great time to be outdoors. You do not have to worry about getting wet, as you would in the rain or the snow. There are hundreds of different things that you can do outside on a sunny day, from reading a book to rock climbing and hiking.

You can lie down in the grass and read a book on a sunny day.

A Nearby Star

As you enjoy the Sun's rays, remember that they traveled over 90 **million** miles (145 million km) to reach you. This is the distance between Earth and the Sun, our nearest star. As all stars are, the Sun is a huge ball of hot gases.

The Sun can be as hot as 28 million° F (16 million° C). This heat allows **atoms** of **hydrogen** to come together and make atoms of **helium**. This makes **energy**. The energy flows out from the center of the Sun. Some of the energy reaches Earth as light and heat.

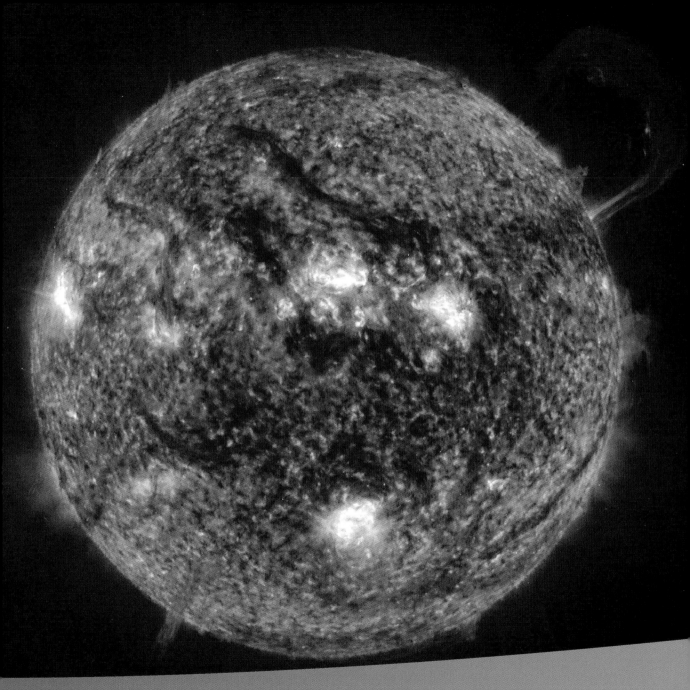

You can see the spinning clouds of hot gas in this close-up photo of the Sun.

Dressing for a Sunny Day

Some of the energy that reaches Earth from the Sun reaches us as ultraviolet rays. Ultraviolet rays are a kind of light that people cannot see. Ultraviolet rays make your skin tanned. If your skin takes in too many ultraviolet rays, it becomes red and it hurts. This is a sunburn.

Make sure to stay safe from ultraviolet rays when you are outside. Always wear **sunscreen**. Try to stay out of direct sunlight in the middle of the day. Spend time in the shade or go out in the late afternoon, instead.

Sunglasses keep your eyes safe from bright light. Many sunglasses block out ultraviolet light, too.

9

Fun in the Sun

Though you must be careful not to get too much sun, there are many things to do on a sunny day. It is a great time to take a walk or a run. Walking and running are fun ways to get exercise. They also offer a chance to enjoy nature.

Sunny days are good times to go boating, too. If you tip over and get wet, you will dry off quickly in the sunlight. Sunny days are also the easiest times to go hiking or ride a bike.

Playing with a remote-controlled boat is one of the many things you can do on a sunny day.

Beach Days

Lots of people enjoy going to the beach in sunny weather. The cool water feels great on a hot, sunny day. Many people like to lie on the sand, read a book, and get a tan. This is an agreeable way to spend a sunny day, but remember to wear sunscreen!

Building sand **castles** is another fun thing to do at the beach. You can gather stones and shells to put on your castle. If you have a group of friends with you, you can make a whole city of sand castles!

Surfing is another fun thing to do at the beach!

Sun Prints

Making **sun prints** is another fun thing to do on a sunny day. Sun prints are made with special paper that has **chemicals** in it that take in light. Lay natural objects, like feathers, leaves, or flowers, on top of the paper. Place them in the sun for several minutes. Run water over the paper to fix the picture.

If you cannot find sun print paper, you can use dark-colored paper. Leave the paper in the sun for at least an hour and do not wash the paper with water.

The family who made this sun print used plants that they found in their garden.

15

Why We Need the Sun

The Sun plays a big part in life on Earth. Plants use sunlight to make the energy they need to live and grow. Animals get the energy they need by eating plants or by eating animals that have eaten plants. All the energy that living things use first came from the Sun.

The Sun also causes all kinds of weather on Earth, not just sunny days. The Sun warms air unevenly, which makes wind. The Sun's warmth causes water to **evaporate**. This evaporated water forms the clouds from which rain and snow fall.

Both this girl and the flower she is picking use energy that came from the Sun.

Solar Power

Along with the energy we need to live, the Sun supplies the power some people use to heat their homes. Power made from the Sun's energy is called solar power. Much of the solar power in the United States is made by solar panels, or plates. Solar panels are often placed on the roof of a house. They change the Sun's energy into power to heat the house.

The Sun also supplies the energy for solar power plants. They use sunlight to make power for many houses. Some cars even run on solar energy!

The solar panels on the roof of this house supply all the energy that the house needs.

Droughts

Solar energy is useful. Sunny days are nice. However, too much sun can cause problems. If the weather stays sunny for too long, a **drought** might happen. Plants dry up during a drought. Animals have trouble finding food.

During a drought people must be careful not to use too much water. Governments often lay down rules about how much water people can use. Sometimes people are allowed to water the grass only at night, when the water will evaporate less. During bad droughts people are not allowed to water their lawns at all.

In 2005, a drought in Spain made this riverbed dry up.
Droughts often cause this kind of dry, broken dirt.

21

The Sun and Earth

Too much sunny weather can cause droughts, but people, plants, and animals all need the Sun. There would be no life on Earth without the Sun. Stars do not last for all time, though. In about five **billion** years, the Sun will use up all its hydrogen. The Sun will grow and swallow up Earth. Then it will grow smaller again and become a kind of star called a white dwarf.

This will not happen for billions of years, though. In the meantime we can keep on enjoying the Sun's light and warmth!

Glossary

atoms (A-temz) The smallest parts into which matter can be broken down.

billion (BIL-yun) 1,000 millions.

castles (KA-sulz) Buildings with high walls.

chemicals (KEH-mih-kulz) Matter that can be mixed with other matter to cause changes.

drought (DROWT) A period of dryness that hurts crops.

energy (EH-nur-jee) The power to work or to act.

evaporate (ih-VA-puh-rayt) To change from a liquid, like water, to a gas, like steam.

helium (HEE-lee-um) A light colorless gas.

hydrogen (HY-dreh-jen) A colorless gas that burns easily.

million (MIL-yun) A very large number.

sun prints (SUN PRINTS) Pictures made by sunlight.

sunscreen (SUN-skreen) A cream that keeps the skin safe from the Sun's harmful rays.

Index

Web Sites

Due to the changing nature of Internet links, PowerKids Press has developed an online list of Web sites related to this book. This site is updated regularly. Please use this link to access the list:
www.powerkidslinks.com/wtw/sunny/